I0526885

WITCH RABBIT 2

Moody Mona and the Vampire in the Witches' Dormitory!

Written by
Kelly Marie Bradley

and

Illustrated by
Louis Hansell

Witch Rabbit 2. Moody Mona and the Vampire in the Witches' Dormitory!
Copyright©2019 by Kelly Marie Bradley and Louis Hansell.

All rights reserved. Printed in the United States of America. No part of this book may be used or reproduced in any manner whatsoever without written permission except in the case of brief quotations embodied in critical articles and reviews. For information, address Louis Hansell. louis.rats@gmail.com.

First New Montgomery Press edition published 2019.

Library of Congress Cataloging-in-Publication Data

Bradley, Kelly Marie
Hansell, Louis
Witch Rabbit 2. Moody Mona and the Vampire in the Witches' Dormitory!
1st New Montgomery Press ed.
ISBN 9-78-0-578-59072-1
New Montgomery Press .

For Ed, Jean, and the Bats...

- Kelly Marie Bradley

For Kelly. The prettiest witch I know.

- Louis Hansell

"For the moon never beams without bringing me dreams."

- Edgar Allan Poe

It was a crisp, calm evening. A huge luminous full moon
was hovering in the sky when Quentin arrived over
Mona's house.

Mona, Stench, and Finicus were dancing and giggling as their music floated out the open window. Filling the fresh autumn air.

Quentin flew towards the music flowing out the window.
The closer he got the faster his wings flapped. His heart
was beating out of his chest with excitement! He swooped
inside and gave the letter to Mona.

Mona, Stench, and Finicus followed Quentin downstairs.
He explained she was invited to the Dame School for Witches.
Then he opened a secret doorway and said, "Follow me, Mona."

"Welcome, Mona! I'm Miss Watson, the head mistress. These are your classmates."

Mona was bubbling with feelings of hullabaloo! She met the
school witches Penelope, Tiffany, Margery and their familiars.

The first day of class the familiars gathered around and enjoyed the Fortune Cupcakes made by their witches. They only tasted good to familiars. The cupcake Margery made for her familiar exploded with a curse!

Mona laid awake all night. Eyes wide. Heart racing. A shadow moved out of the corner of her eyes. She looked up and saw Stench in the window. One of her classmates was missing!

Mona got out of bed and went outside into the full moonlight.
She saw Stench attack her classmate Penelope and they
disappeared into thin air! Mona was frozen in shock.

The next day Mona sat tired and distracted in class.
Miss Watson told a strange tale about the Dame sisters
who founded the Witch House.

There were once three witches...

And one of them unleashed a terrible curse!

Late that evening, Mona went for a walk to clear her head.
She saw Margery lunged upon by a snarling werewolf!

Count Stench seemed to appear out of nowhere and fought off the werewolf!

The missing witch Penelope had returned and grabbed Tiffany.
Mona noticed she had stolen the Evil Spell Book previously owned
by the Dame Sisters. Which belonged to Head Mistress Watson.

Quentin swooped down, swiped the book out of Penelope's hands, and Mona grabbed it. She read a spell and cast Penelope into The Goblin Witch Dimension!

"At last! The curse is lifted!", Miss Watson declared.

"I couldn't have done it without the help of Count Stench and Finicus. I asked them to keep an eye on Penelope. I suspected she was trying to steal the Book of Dame to unleash an ancient evil. Thank you, Mona!"

Mona, Stench, and Finicus said their goodbyes and stepped through the gateway back to their home.

Mona finished up her week at Witch School where she got all A's. She was grateful to be home with Stench & Finicus, watching horror movies. Quentin brought his favorite, garlic pizza! Mona was alone for 18 years but her family of misfits was growing. She never felt happier!

THE END?

www.ingramcontent.com/pod-product-compliance
Lightning Source LLC
Chambersburg PA
CBHW041002170626

46815CB00002B/113